The Goat

Written by Jill Eggleton
Illustrated by Jan van der Voo

The goat
ate the apples.

Gobble,
gobble,
gobble!

Gobble, gobble,
gobble!

3

The goat
ate the flowers.

Gobble,
gobble,
gobble!

Gobble, gobble,
gobble!

5

The goat
ate the book.

6

Gobble,
gobble,
gobble!

Gobble, gobble, gobble!

7

The goat
ate the sock.

Gobble, gobble, gobble!

Gobble, gobble, gobble!

9

The goat
ate the soap.

Gobble, gobble,
gobble!

Bubble, bubble, bubble

12

bubble, bubble, bubble!

A List

apples

flowers

book

sock

soap

▬▬ Guide Notes

Title: The Goat

Stage: Emergent – Magenta

Genre: Fiction

Approach: Guided Reading

Processes: Thinking Critically, Exploring Language, Processing Information

Written and Visual Focus: List, Item Box

READING THE TEXT

Tell the children that the story is about a goat who goes into a house and gobbles things. Talk to them about what is on the front cover. Read the title and the author / illustrator. "Walk" through the book, focusing on the illustrations and talking to the children about the different rooms the goat goes into and what it gobbles.

Before looking at pages 12 - 13, ask the children to make a prediction.

Read the text together.

THINKING CRITICALLY

(sample questions)

*   Why do you think the goat went into the house instead of staying outside?
*   How do you think the goat will get rid of all those bubbles?

EXPLORING LANGUAGE

(ideas for selection)

Terminology

Title, cover, author, illustrator, illustrations

Vocabulary

Interest words: goat, gobble, apples, flowers, book, sock, soap, bubble

High-frequency word: the